The Marriage Wars

By Lin Morris

For Alex...

The Look in Their Eyes

Our wedding picture sits on the northwest corner of my desk.

I'm one of the very few here with a desk to call my own; at least it's mine for eight hours, Monday through Saturday. Someone else may use it after I leave, I don't know. I don't have any idea if there's a swing shift or a graveyard shift here. I don't think so, but I don't ask. It's something I worked very diligently to achieve, my desk, earned with nose kept both down and clean, eyes reverentially averted. Eyes *never* where they don't belong.

My desk is a tiny four feet by two feet, plain wood top, not even painted, just a thin varnish to keep it workably smooth. On it sits the picture, a phone, and my computer screen and keyboard. I have a blotter which I am required periodically—when ordered—to pick up by the outer sides, to prove I've got nothing hidden under it. Depending on how by-the-book the Boss doing the ordering, I might have to shake it out, to prove I've got nothing hidden between its monthly calendar pages. I never hide anything. I don't disobey the rules.

Well. Except for this one thing, the glorious ten minutes I get to myself two days a week, when I'm typing up the production totals (Tuesdays) and the outgoing product report (Fridays) on a spreadsheet. During those ten minutes, when Boss A confers with Boss B in the latter's office, talking about I don't know what (but always for a strict ten minutes only), most days I use my time to type up my little thoughts on life.

Like what I'm typing now, my instant disposable diary-slash-autobiography. Which I delete as soon as Boss A stands up from his chair in Boss B's office. Good thing there's a window, so I have warning. Writing it up helps me make sense of things, though; for twenty minutes a week, the world is mine. I wish there were some way to save these musings, but I don't know if this computer is monitored.

When they first brought me into the office, after it became obvious I have absolutely no proficiency at manual labor or production line, I lied about my words per minute typing ability. I low-balled the number, just to cover myself in case they wanted more than I could give them. So, while it allegedly takes me thirty-ish minutes to type up notes and totals, in truth it takes me only twenty-ish minutes. And for ten minutes, I am left to my own devices.

You know, when it became obvious that I have absolutely no skill or proficiency at manual labor and production line, they could have simply killed me on the spot. Others have been killed for as little or less.

But, as it turned out, I was familiar with the antiquated software program they use to track warehouse production and efficiency. It's so old I didn't know it even existed anymore. I had used it at a part-time job I had during my junior and senior years of high school.

So anyway, my wedding picture. Why did I waste most of today's ten minutes writing about my desk? It's not like anyone will ever actually read this. Right? Unless, maybe, somehow, just by typing it, somehow it goes into the whatever, ether, atmosphere, wherever these things go when typed up on a word processor before being deleted. Maybe someone is somewhere on the receiving end. Maybe you. Are You reading this right now, somewhere?

The wedding picture. Betsy's and mine. Prisoner 34 and Mrs. 34; these are our official names now. The simple wedding costumes, a dark suit jacket and tie and a plain white gown, were split up the back, like something designed to dress a body for the casket. We slipped our arms through the sleeves over the clothes we had on and an Officer zipped us up. It added about ten pounds to our frames, which wasn't a bad thing after almost a year of near-starvation. Someone handed Betsy a dusty bouquet of silk flowers. They didn't even give her real roses for what was, they told us over and over, a magical day. But it's required, the photo, they made us take it when they united us in holy matrimony, me and Betsy.

We are smiling, our eyes bright and glistening with what only the willfully naïve would mistake for tears of happiness. Anyone with half a brain can see our eyes are dewy with fear and desperation.

The One Uncontrollable Thing

You'd think after all this time, just over six years now, I'd be able to orient myself more quickly when I gasp awake from a bad dream. But I can't. I wake up from bad dreams, which I still have from time to time (though not as often as I did at first), and there is always that horrible few seconds when I don't know where I am or what's going on, my throat dry and my mouth tasting sour, like when you get a paper cut and you stick your finger in your mouth and suck the razor-thin line of blood. A hot coppery aftertaste. Betsy will often instinctively reach out and put her thick arm across my chest, not always even awake when she does it, but sensing the sudden shift of my body as it inflates with alarm and adrenaline.

My bad dreams aren't nightmares, they're just regular dreams. What makes them bad is they're always about Dylan. While it's not always the same exact dream, it's usually some variation of a recurring scenario. We're sitting out on the back deck of the house I don't own anymore, the house that was foreclosed or stolen or whatever constitutes the proper terminology for what happened to it. What really happened is, my lovely house was *storm-troopered*, except that's not actually a verb. In fact, when I wrote that just now, a red squiggly line instantly appeared right beneath it, so I clicked the "Add to Dictionary" command for future use. I don't like a red squiggly line telling me what I know to be true is invalid.

So my house was storm-troopered. They came bursting in unannounced, their whistles and flashlights destroying the perfect symmetry of silence and darkness that normally accompanies the four a.m. predawn. Even in the dim light, the metal of their weapons gleamed.

But back to the bad dreams, the variations of a single theme: we sit on the back deck, usually in the purple bruise of dusk, my favorite time to sit outside. And we just talk. The conversations are so real, perhaps recollections of the very conversations we had once upon a time, full of trivia like picking up milk at the store or getting new shocks for my car. I never remember the details of the conversation when I wake up from the dreams, panting and sweating and full of copper, only that it was inconsequential.

If I'm going to dream about the past, why can't it be full of import and epic in theme? Dramatic! There's a word I used to love. The one thing I can't control is the content of my dreams. Why is it all, "I can't remember if I gave the cat her worm medicine this morning, do you think it'll hurt to give her a double does tonight?"

Simple stuff like that. What makes it a bad dream is seeing Dylan in it.

I never saw him again after that night, when the house was storm-troopered. Well. Maybe one time, but I'll most likely never know for sure if it was him.

I never saw the cat again, for that matter, fluffy old Tabitha.

I certainly never saw my house again.

What did they do with the houses they took? Sell them? Live in them? Or were they afraid our houses were infected? Did they march forward shouting threats, like the torch-wielding villagers coming after Frankenstein's monster, and burn our houses to the ground?

The Herb-Crusted Chicken is a Success

These are the days my heart hurts the most: when I come in after a long day at work and I see Betsy in the kitchen, leaning over the counter or the stove, and the slumped posture of her wide-ish backside radiates defeat.

It doesn't happen every day. There are days she finds something akin to happiness in the creation of our nightly meal. The recipe works; our unreliable oven decides to not randomly up the temp by twenty degrees; and her lone specialty, Herb-Crusted Chicken, is not scorched.

They made Betsy take several weeks of cooking classes, back when *she* was storm-troopered. Couldn't cook a lick then, never liked to and so never did; she was always, she says on the rare occasions when she talks about the past, mistress of the take out menu.

On the good-cooking days when everything has gone right, she will hear me come in and will turn to welcome me from across the ridiculously tiny apartment and her voice will be upbeat and maybe on the best day even exuberant, and she will say, "Dinner will be ready in twenty minutes." Or ten minutes. Or an hour. However long is left for me to relax after the day at work I've had, which on the best day is tense and leaves me with an almost-headache. Her smile is genuinely pretty, despite the unflattering shade of regulation lipstick, which she is forever getting on her teeth. In her moments of greatest concentration, she bites her lip. I've spent what feels like a full one-tenth of our marriage brushing my teeth with my index finger to bring it to her attention.

   On those good days, when everything has gone right, my heart breaks just the regular amount.

Something Funny Happens

"Huh," said Dylan one night, "that's weird." Dark eyes brewing, furrowed brow, clicking away at his laptop.

"Hmm?" I was only paying half attention. Was I cleaning up after dinner, maybe? Watching TV? Odd how an event so momentous is fuzzy in the details. You'd think I would remember every second of it. But it was only important in retrospect.

"There was an article I found this morning and didn't have time to read, so I saved it for later." Something political, no doubt, from one of the websites he favored, all squawking outrage and calls for unity and protest.

I was not political, not in the way you think of when you hear the word. Living my life was political by example (I told myself and everyone else), and that was good enough for me.

"And…?" I said. Perhaps I was unloading the dishwasher?

"I keep getting an error message for the web address."

"Maybe you're entering it wrong." Feeding the cat?

"I'm not entering it *wrong*, I'm clicking the link and it doesn't exist anymore. *I saved the article.*"

It creeps me out now, to think that as we went about our daily lives, people were conducting secret meetings, decisions were being made, and laws were being drafted. And they were so quiet about it, too.

A couple of days later, the brand new Department of Public Knowledge took over the media, and a couple of days after that, there was no such thing as the internet. And then came the rest.

We didn't even see it coming.

No. *I* didn't see it coming. Dylan knew to worry, his blessing and possibly his curse.

Three Little Words

    I haven't written in over two weeks. Doing so now makes me nervous.

    Stupid mistake, so basic that I never even thought to come up with a contingency plan. I was typing up my report on a Tuesday when Boss A suddenly popped up out of his chair in Boss B's office, super fast and unexpected, not to mention nearly four minutes early, and just like that poked his head out of the door and said, "34, I need that report."

    "It's not quite finished, Sir," I said with proper respect, my eyes downcast and resolutely not at the finger I had glued to the backspace key, deleting-deleting-deleting.

    "I'll take what you got so far," he said. When I didn't hop fast enough I guess, he added an exasperated, "Now, 34."

    He was at my desk in seconds. I deleted almost all of it before he got there, but with him standing right next to me I had no choice but to hit Print.

    I left only three words undeleted, "We went to." Cut short and out of context, but unmistakably prose after a third-page of rows and columns listing product numbers and quantities and dates. There was no way for the boss to not see it. He ripped the wide report paper from the printer at the perforation and walked back to the inner office, head bowed, reading. His precise military stride faltered so briefly, if you weren't looking for it you wouldn't have noticed. But I saw it alright, the curiosity in the slight rise of his shoulders, how he ducked his head a couple of inches closer to the report to reread what stood out as a glaring error.

"We went to."

I kept my face pointed to the monitor, but even in subtle side eye it was obvious they were both staring out at me from Boss B's office. Boss A was back in less than a minute, suddenly very busy two or three feet from my desk, making a great show of cleaning the counter, straightening the calendar, doing all the tedious tasks he usually sloughs off to me. He sharpened pencils, so help me. And every time he turned my direction, his hand would slip to fondle the gun strapped to his belt. A reminder to me, I think, of who's in charge here. He "randomly" asked me to lift my blotter, to shake out the calendar pages and thus prove my innocence.

It's a miracle I remembered to type slowly, at my fake speed, until the report was finished.

It's a miracle I was able to type at all, really. The terror sweat kept causing my fingers to slip from the keys.

Their eyes were on me—sometimes subtly, often blatantly—for the next few days. Only a fool would have tried to get away with something. I probably shouldn't be risking it now. I had to type very slowly, to fill the entire thirty-ish minutes. That was agonizing. It gave me cramps in my middle knuckles, the way I used to get them when I was a teenager and my piano teacher Mrs. Sharp (I swear!) would assign a complex practice piece to see if I was ready to bump up to the next level, only this time I didn't get a beautiful melody for my troubles.

Contingency plan for the next time: X out of whatever I'm doing, immediately.

Of course it will mean losing all my work, but what are they going to do? The only thing left for them to take from me is my life, and technically, they've already done that. They just haven't taken my *aliveness* yet.

I miss playing the piano so much.

Sometimes, when I type, in my head I hear which notes the keys should be.

Frederick 1

"Which?" said Frederick, holding one topsider in each hand. "Neon yellow or tri-color?"

If a love of shoes were the core basis for true romance, Frederick and I would have been soul mates for life. Instead we were great friends and shameless shoe whores. In fact, we first met when we both reached for the last pair of the previous season's size 9 Armani monkstraps on the clearance shelf. Frederick winked slyly and said, "If this were a rom-com, we'd have bonked heads." (While I giggled like a doofus at his sexy British accent, he snapped up the shoes.)

"Neither," I said with my patented sneer. "On trend or not, topsiders are *never* acceptable."

Frederick gave me his signature eye roll. "Good thing, then, they aren't for you."

"I don't care if it *is* your birthday, I'm not paying for topsiders." But of course I did. It's the whole reason we were shoe shopping that day.

His birthday wasn't the last time I saw Frederick, but it was the last *good* time. All the bad stuff was a mere nine days away.

The Word That Means the Opposite of Taut

On Wednesdays, Betsy greets me just inside the door when I get home, my robe in her hand. I'd lost track of the days of the week, I guess, because how can it be Wednesday again already? My mind has been on work, I guess, on covering my dreadful "We went to" mistake by acting as normal as possible.

Normal. How many times did I hear that word in the early days? Normal! Always hissed at us angrily. They loved to toss it around, their favorite buzzword, so newly Officially Sanctioned.

Betsy handed me my robe, making small talk as we moved across the room to the out-of-date stacked washer and dryer set. She always does this on laundry day. I took off my regulation under- and outer shirts and threw them in the washer, then slipped my arms through the robe. I killed a few more seconds by removing my socks first. But then there's no choice but to pull off my black pants. Black is slimming! Who used to always say that, which of my friends? "Black is slimming!" Awful what I can't remember; but really it's what I will myself to forget. And finally my regulation underwear (traditional tighty-whiteys, of course). Betsy is calm and silent, hands resting atop the bottom half of the machine, eyes fixed on the wall slightly to her left. It's a studio bungalow, there's really nowhere else to go. What am I gonna do, change in the bathroom? But I appreciate the effort she makes to allow me some dignity. She never looks down, though I've got nothing she hasn't seen before. In the old days she was a nurse; my nudity wouldn't faze her.

It fazes me, though, how out of shape and ungroomed I have become. Not fat, which is almost a genetic impossibility for me, but fleshy, without tone. What is the opposite of taut? That's what I am.

"Thanks," I said, relieved and embarrassed.

"Oh, of course," she said, then gave me a sweet smile. I didn't indicate to her that she had lipstick on her teeth. "My pleasure." She tossed in a detergent packet and gave the knob of the machine a slap with the palm of her hand. The machines they gave us are all old styles, nothing with push buttons or remote controls. Usable, but just.

I started to turn away, but caught the little sag in her face as her smile faded. It was enough to pull me back. I reached around her broad shoulders and gave her a tight hug.

"Sorry," I whispered softly. "For all of this."

We never know if they're listening or not. The levels of their monitoring have always been kept vague, a threat wafting vaporously over our daily lives, keeping us off balance.

"I know," she whispered back. "I know you are. Me, too."

"We can do this," I said into her ear.

"Okay," she said, and pulled out of the embrace enough to look me in the eye. "We can do this."

She really is a good person. I don't mind that she's close to ten years older than me, already in her mid-to-late-40s.

I could have done a lot worse in the Wife Lottery.

The New Freedom

It's so strange, on the rare occasions when I must leave the office and go out into the factory—accompanied by a Good Guy, of course—and no one says anything. All the men stand at their machines, or on the assembly line, spaced apart the distance of a double arm span, everyone working, no one looking at each other, the armed Good Guys constantly watching. And above the whirs and clanks of the machinery is this eerie. . .nothing. The silent lunch breaks are even creepier.

The No Talking rule is the rule I think I hate the most. I speak to Bosses A and B, when spoken to first and only on business matters, and Betsy and I can talk a blue streak at home when the mood hits us. Talking with your spouse is not only allowed but encouraged.

I don't know why they don't simply have guards (sorry: Good Guys) do the running back and forth. It seems silly to accompany me across the yard and into the factory, or to bring one of the workers into the office and have a Good Guy stand mutely by, especially since the Bosses monitor our every word anyway. I imagine it's some sort of test, to see if close proximity will somehow get the better of us, cause us to tear off our clothes.

Because we're all victims of our "uncontrollable desires." Perhaps you've heard.

Do they secretly hope we'll suddenly fly into each other's arms? Some of them must itch to pick us off for sport the way they were allowed to for the first year.

It took those in charge that long to realize a giant dormitory setting was self-defeating to their purpose; everyone caught "comingling with your fellow prisoner" was killed immediately, often right in mid-act. If I hadn't been awakened by so many death screams, I could almost believe they died happy.

At least the activation of the Marriage Lottery got us into our own little bungalow apartments, humble though they might be. The death toll dropped by half inside of two months.

But the gift of our lives, allowed us once the Humane Laws were put into effect, took from us freedoms I don't think we realized weren't a given: the freedom to converse; to make eye contact; to smile, or to have any expression on our faces besides blank and passive supplication.

In exchange, we stay alive. I can't speak for the rest of the country, but here, wherever it is we are (Betsy's guess, based on humidity, is the lower southeast, probably Georgia), I estimate about only thirty per cent of those I first arrived with are still living.

We're calm, quiet, docile. We're made to dress in the plainest clothes your mind can conjure. Our shoes are nothing but functional.

But we live. Prisoner 34 is still alive, while so many others aren't.

On Missing Holidays

Because I work in the office, I have daily access to the calendar. Otherwise, I don't think I would ever know the date. I mean, we're all aware of the days of the week, because they give us Sundays off—though why I don't know, it's not like we're allowed to leave our homes and socialize. All Sunday means is we're stuck sitting around with nothing to break the monotony; the closed-circuit television doesn't play anything on Sundays.

Knowing the date is in some ways comforting, but every time a holiday rolls around, my pain doubles. I am always aware of my birthday, and Dylan's, and those of my family and close friends. Even Betsy's. Whatever the special day, I'm aware that I'm not celebrating it.

We've never celebrated Christmas here, and only ever had the day off if it fell on a Sunday.

Oh, Halloween, how I miss you the most! Every Halloween, I wear mismatched socks and secretly pretend it's my costume. They only give us dark black socks and dark blue socks, so the difference is subtle. But I know it's there.

Frederick 2

The last time I saw Frederick was by complete chance, three days after The Reckoning. They had herded a huge group of us straight off the train and into a large hangar and put us in a long, roped-off line which we followed back and forth like we were waiting our turn to ride a theme park's most popular attraction. As we waited for nobody-knew-what, the guards paraded up and down the rows with their rifles; we didn't call them Good Guys then, that law hadn't been passed down to us yet, though of course we knew from the news stories in the pre-coup days that that's what they called themselves. In the middle of each pass, Frederick and I met up across the rope from each other, he in the row behind me. We let our hands touch quickly along the rope and whispered our frantic questions. No, he hadn't seen Dylan; no, I hadn't seen Michael.

"What are they doing?" he whispered at me on our second meeting across the rope. I shrugged, giving side eye to the guards marching at the end of the row. It reminded me of the footage I'd seen on the news five months before, when the new government had deported all the Mexicans. Supposedly, they were only after the Illegals, but then of course American-born Mexicans of illegal parents and even grandparents were deported, too. The resulting protests brought about no change, unless you count the increase of protesters who ended up in jail.

Up ahead, at the front of the line, they were separating us into two groups, a small group behind a makeshift fence on the left and the majority of us in a larger open area to the right. There was no way to definitively guess which group you wanted to be in, but that fenced area couldn't be good.

We continued to move slowly until at last I got to the head of the line. There were four desks set up, and at each sat a man in a white doctor's coat. Each doctor had a large box of cotton swabs enclosed in plastic hoods. They were those "Insta-Status" kits that had been developed a few years earlier; every gay man was familiar with them. One of the gunmen motioned me forward.

"Open your mouth," said the doctor matter-of-factly. I did as instructed. He pulled one of the swabs from its plastic hood and stuck it in my mouth between gum and cheek. I glanced back in the line. Frederick's eyes got wide with recognition and fear.

"They're testing for HIV," he said. He looked around, panicked, at all the other prisoners. "You see what they're doing? They're testing us for AIDS!" His voice was contemptuous and loud, and echoed slightly in the cavernous space. As he turned face front, the butt of a Good Guy's assault rifle cracked across his face and he went down in a heap.

Two of them grabbed him under the armpits and pulled him roughly forward.

"You got a reason to be worried?" one of them said.

Frederick had been positive but healthy as long as I'd known him. He used to love to tease me, saying he was "so disgustingly healthy it puts you to shame. You should get HIV so you can be as healthy as me!"

But now, for the first time, his status made me very afraid.

He brought a hand up to his mouth and looked at the blood staining his fingertips. He looked at the guard; he looked over at me and smiled.

The doctor pulled the swab from my mouth so suddenly I jumped. "Negative!" he said, smiling almost proudly. I was ushered to the area on the right. Suddenly the reason for the fenced area on the left made scary sense.

"Worried?" Frederick said to the guard around a mouthful of blood, his accent no longer regal but rounder, working-class. "You're the one who should worry, mate."

Frederick spat a glob of bloody saliva into the guard's face. Then he laughed out loud, one quick "Haha!"

They shot Frederick immediately, right in front of all of us.

They took the spat-on Good Guy away. I hope they shot him, too, in their fear and stupidity.

The doctor looked at me again, the proud smile gone, the replacement hate in his eyes daring me to say something, to cry, to react.

I knew right then I wanted to live.

I'd gladly be a coward if it meant I could go on living. Just like before, my life would be a silent political act, but this time the political act meant surrendering to the enemy. So I did my best to not react.

And neither did I react—well, not much—when the Good Guys gunned down the rest of the positive men in the group on the left a half hour later.

I choose to think when Frederick looked at me and smiled one last time, it was his goodbye rather than a challenge for me to follow suit and rebel, but I'll never know. I had no idea he was so brave, but I think he knew I was cowardly.

The List of Better Lives

A lot of things were worse at first; I remind myself of that on days like today, when the general unhappiness to which I've become quite accustomed degenerates into something deeper, darker, insinuating its tendrils into my bloodstream. To keep from going crazy on days like today, I list all the ways in which life is better than it was five years ago, when they moved us all here.

1. While technically still prisoners, at least we're in our own bungalow apartment homes instead of actual camps. Most days I can will myself to forget the camp where I spent the first year. On top of the constant fear, the gunfire, the lack of food, what stays with me is the crushing boredom. We didn't have jobs then, we just sat around and remembered our former lives. It was a year of living inside my own head, which was the same as living in hell.

2. I have a job which, even though we're not paid anything, gives me something to do for 48 of the 168 hours of each week.

3. Last year they gave us all crappy, outmoded TVs and began offering us one channel of closed-circuit television each

evening from six until ten o'clock. Much of its content consists of panels of talking heads telling us why we're bad people who brought this on ourselves, but they've begun to show reruns of very old sitcoms featuring traditional families and a "wholesome" classic movie each Saturday night at eight. One night a few months ago they played an old ghost story called *The Uninvited*. Betsy immediately leaned in and whispered, "Lesbian cult movie." We had the best time watching that one, cuddled together on the couch so she could decode all the subtle Sapphic messages in my ear, feeling like we'd put something over on a clueless programmer. The movie's never been repeated, so maybe they figured it out. Or perhaps the supernatural content was ruled unacceptable.

4. When it finally became obvious, despite all their valiant efforts, that the majority of the prisoners did not wish to stop being gay, those in charge eventually suspended the mandatory Reorientation Classes we were forced to attend every single night (official motto: "Change Your Life!"). Some elected to try and Change Their Lives, though whether they did so out of genuine desire or fear of punishment I cannot say. It's not as though deciding to become straight afforded them any more

luxury or easier living than the rest of us. They remained prisoners, living in the barracks apartments with their same old Lottery-assigned, opposite-sex spouses, working in the factory (the men) or as a homemaker (the women). I still see those men when we march to work each morning. We all still meet with our personal Mentors once a week, but there's less pressure now. They've adopted a "Lead by Example" approach these days.

5. As part of the Humane Laws, they no longer force us to have sex with our spouses once a month while they watch. It was deemed unnecessarily cruel. You don't know performance anxiety until you've had it in front of someone holding a gun.

These are things I list to console myself on days like today, which happens to be Dylan's birthday.

Dylan who might be alive.

The Important Thing You Should Know

You do realize, don't You, that Betsy isn't her real name? That Dylan is an alias? As is Frederick, for that matter.

Because if You do exist and are reading this, and if You are one of the bad guys, I don't want You to hurt them.

P.S. fyi, I even made up the name of my old cat.

Passing

Despite my very gay penchant for show tunes, I've never been particularly flamboyant.

People would express surprise when I said things like "My partner" or, after our wedding, "My husband." They'd give their little "Oh!" of shock, and I would wonder what I did to misrepresent myself. Clearly my sexuality didn't proclaim its persuasion to others. Even my family was shocked—or as shocked as it was possible for them to be—when I came out at Thanksgiving dinner during my sophomore year of college (except my younger brother, whose response through a mouthful of marshmallowed yams was, "I could have told you that!"). Which disappointed me: how much of my youth had I wasted being fearful that my every gesture and vocal inflection was betraying me?

Anyway, my point is, I always wanted to be, well, *gayer* than I appear. More stereotypical, so there would be no mistake. I could never pull it off, apparently. The common refrain was, "Why, I had no idea!"

I complained about this once over lunch with my dear friend Bernadette, who replied, with confusion that equaled my own, "They have heard you *talk*, right?"

"Thank you! That's what I say!"

"People are stupid," she said, and we clinked our martini glasses in smug solidarity.

It probably goes without saying, but I no longer try to act gayer than I naturally do. They're on to me anyway or I wouldn't be here.

Number 34

The day they officially closed our camp, we were loaded into the open beds of several large trucks. No one said where we were going or what was happening. Almost immediately, a prisoner in the second truck jumped out and began running furiously across an open field. The Good Guys didn't even bother to shout a warning before they shot him, which fed our speculation that this ride would end in our mass slaughter. This was before the No Talking rule was initiated, so we openly weighed the possibilities. Several of the men in my truck were weeping, while others tried to figure out how we could overtake the Good Guys.

After travelling a few more miles, the trucks pulled off the highway and through the open gate of a huge, fenced-in compound. It was a deserted army barracks. Hung over the entrance was a hand-painted wooden sign designating this simply as "Factory."

Once we were inside, the convoy drove around to the back side of the property. We came to a stop beside an equal number of trucks containing the women prisoners, and we all stared across at each other blankly. Right away they herded us off the trucks. The Officers who helped us down were safely sheathed in thick rubber gloves, as though to touch our flesh would somehow either infect them or incite our lust. As we each jumped to the ground, a different Officer pointed a finger in our faces and shouted a number at us, along with a warning that we were not to forget our number; failure to respond to our number could result in severe but unspecified punishment. I was Number 34.

They lined us up according to number in six rows each of men and women. Good Guys surrounded us, guns at the ready.

From a low building across the way, a man in more formal military wear emerged and looked over the two groups on either side of him. He stepped into the open grassy space between us, introduced himself as our Administrator, and shouted "1!"

The man at the far left of the front row raised his hand and took a cautious, confused step forward. A woman from the row opposite us stepped forward as well. They stood staring at each other for a second or two until a gloved Officer swooped in and guided them by the shoulders toward a large barracks building behind my group. We all swiveled our heads and watched them march off to who-knows-what manner of certain death.

"2!" shouted the Administrator.

And so we moved through the two groups. I kept trying to find my distaff 34, but every time I thought I had her pegged, the line shifted or a very short woman I hadn't noticed stepped forward and I had to start over. When finally my group was at the front, I counted down the row until my finger came to rest at a tall, broad-bodied woman with a thick, wavy mass of untamable hair carpeting the lace collar of her drab navy blue dress. You could see from the way she kept tugging it fruitlessly back out of her face that she was unused to such an abundance of hair and probably had, in her freedom days, kept it short. She was clearly burdened by the constraints of clothes and coif, and my heart broke for her without hesitation. At least they mercifully let the women wear flats.

Finally: "34!"

Having learned from thirty-three previous examples, the woman and I moved directly into the center and allowed ourselves to be guided to the door of the mystery barracks.

"What'dya suppose this is all about?" she said to me from the corner of her mouth as we approached the building. She seemed almost oddly bemused at the proceedings.

"I wouldn't hazard a guess," I said.

She turned slightly toward me and extended a hand.

"My name's Betsy," she said. We stepped up onto the low porch.

I shook her hand, told her my name, and then a Good Guy opened the door and ushered us through.

Why Dylan Might Not Be Alive

Dylan turned me down the first time I asked him out. When I asked him why later, after we were together, he said I was too "straight-acting" for his tastes at the time. He assumed I was in the closet or else one of the Sporty Frat Gay types he couldn't stand. You know the ones; they'd be in the club wearing their salmon-colored shorts and asking if anyone knew the final score of whatever game was on that evening. Dylan was suspicious of them, as though their love for football and lack of due reverence for dance music and camp made them betrayers of the community. It's not like he paraded around in sequins and tiaras, but you could usually peg Dylan as gay inside of ninety seconds; and if you didn't guess, he'd be sure to tell you.

It's this determination of his that gives me hope for all of us. He's probably in one of the factory barracks somewhere, right this minute planning the revolution. On the flip side of that coin, though, I can't see him bowing his head and doing as he's told, so they probably killed him years ago just to shut him up.

Brother Rita

My Mentor's name is Brother J____. They're all Brother somebody. Meeting with him once a week is something I dread, and yet during the actual meeting I'm always surprised to realize I don't mind it that much. I don't dislike him. His sincerity is rather sweet, and he's certainly cute, though his penchant for dressing like an outdated preppy is laughable. It's the *idea* of the meeting I dislike, of being forced to have a Mentor at all.

One nice thing is, our Mentors come to our homes alone to retrieve us. It's odd to walk alongside another man, free to openly converse. And though a Good Guy is stationed every ten yards or so down the gravel road, they don't bother us. It's just me and Brother J____ from my little bungalow to the Admin Building which houses his office. I guess the Mentors' status comes with privileges.

But not too many: I still have to slide my ID under the glass partition to the man on the other side of the counter when we enter the building, and the interiors of the six Mentor offices are visible on a large monitor behind him, lest heaven forbid something untoward should happen in them. Though we prisoners are being monitored, so too, it seems, are our Mentors. After all, they are ex-gay men; the "gay" overrides the "ex," I guess.

And Brother J____, no matter how strongly he wants to stress his ex-ness, is gay. Like, *gay*-gay. Nobody ever expressed surprise when *he* used words like partner or husband, I bet. His gestures are big, his voice precise and dramatic, and his facial expressions reminiscent of the old Hollywood goddesses; Joan Crawford's got nothing on this guy. He could never pass or be mistaken for something other than what he is, even though he married a woman several years before it was required by law and now has three children. So he's had sex with his wife at least three times. Big deal; so have I.

Though we never knew each other in the past, we lived in the same city and I'd seen him more than a few times at My Queendom, this drag club Bernadette and I used to frequent. We'd go after work on Tuesdays for their three-dollar margaritas. This is back when Brother J____ was better known as Rita Magazine; Rita's specialty was lip-synching to old Doris Day recordings. I only saw Rita out of drag two or three times, sitting at the bar having a cocktail, but at a remove of more than a decade, and without the makeup and the blonde beehive wigs and the bright 60s-era shifts, I know it's him. It takes conscious effort not to slip and call him Brother Rita, which is how I always refer to him in my head. Once I thought of the name, I could never *not* think it, you know? If he knows I know who he is (or was), he never lets on. As far as I can tell, to him I'm just Prisoner 34.

Instead, he begins each meeting by asking politely if he can pray for me. I don't have a problem with that. While I'm not exactly a confident believer, I'm not really a disbeliever, either. The faith I was raised in is, treat others kindly and don't be a jerk. Though God was never disparaged or His existence doubted, He was kind of indirectly involved in our daily lives, more conceptual and much less hands-on.

If there's a chance Brother Rita's prayers will help, why should I object to them? He's genuinely trying to do good. This I believe. His prayers for me aren't the same as my prayers for me, though I think we're both praying for my salvation, in our own ways.

Where Were You?

For people of my parents' generation, the question was always, "Where were you when President Kennedy got shot?" I'm sure my generation, those who are free, ask, "Where were you when President Jansen was assassinated and the Reclamation Party took over?" And that's a legitimate question.

But for me and the people like me, our question right from the start was, "Where were you when Mayor Gomez got shot?" We asked it of everyone we talked to, already sensing its importance in an historical timeline which hadn't played out yet.

Ordinarily, the Pride festivities of another city, especially a city smaller than mine, wouldn't have even been on my radar. But who didn't read about it when, for the first time in history, the protestors at a Pride event outnumbered the participants? The gun-toting open carry brigade, with their famous yellow "We're The *Good Guys*" signs, decided to stand in solidarity with their fellow Antis, to "protect" them from potential harm by us, the celebrants. Apparently, our glitter and jock straps and rainbow flags were the height of violent aggression.

As they were ever reminding us, "*People* kill people, not guns." But sometimes it's just Person, singular; it only takes one. One person to decide he's had enough and take random shots into the crowd at a Pride celebration. After it became clear what was happening and the crowd exploded into screams and chaos, the other Good Guys began shooting their semi-automatic weapons into the air; they didn't kill anyone, but by shooting all together, they created a sound cover which hid the identity and location of the actual shooter.

One of the key members of the Good Guys organization issued a statement the next day, half-heartedly condemning the violence but saying they completely understood the revulsion and actions of the gunman. The audience was full of people with guns and like minds, cheering so loudly the assembled reporters had trouble hearing the speaker's exact words. Not one newspaper quoted him the same way.

That was when the Reclamation Party took up the cause as a social issue. And it was when the public finally understood (long after Dylan had figured it out) that the Reclamation Party was not the unsupported joke we all at first assumed them to be.

Of course, the mayor of the city was outraged. Mayor Gomez held her own press conference, decrying the violence that ensued ("Six people are dead for no other reason but one sick person's irrational hatred of their sexuality!") and also the rain of gunfire that hid the shooter's location. She called for the police to arrest them all. "Since it's impossible to guess just who did the killing," she shouted into the microphone, "let's charge them all with murder! Are they proud enough to stand with their fellows at the expense of their own lives spent in prison?!"

If you saw the local, live news footage, you know the red dot appeared so quickly on her forehead, there wasn't even time to warn her. It was like "blip, BOOM!" before her brains were splattered all over live television.

And then came the inevitable ocean of gunfire, drowning out the location of the shooter.

I was waiting in line for my dry cleaning when the non-live film was played on the news, with Mayor Gomez's exploding head blessedly pixilated. The event was shocking enough on its own, but what really frightened me was the man behind me in line, who muttered, "About friggin' time. Kill them all."

I don't know if by "*them all*" he meant gays, politicians, Latinas, or whom. As I bolted out the door with my dress shirts, I didn't stop to ask.

So that's where I was.

Where were you?

The Right to Refuse Service

As so often happens, the first restaurant Dylan and I went to together kind of became *our* restaurant. It was nothing fancy, about one step up from a diner, but they served the best German Chocolate cake you will ever eat in your entire life. The slices were practically the size of a paperback copy of *Moby Dick*. It was so popular that they sometimes ran out, so we always ordered it before our entrees to make sure we had a reserved slice to share later.

Here was the first odd thing: we went there for our anniversary, reserved the slice of cake, and placed our dinner order. We told the elderly waitress it was our anniversary, but she seemed to not understand, or paid no attention to it; either way, she offered no best wishes. At the end of the meal she brought us two pieces of cake on two separate plates.

"Oh, we just wanted one piece to share," I said.

The waitress leaned in slightly and dropped her voice down to just above a whisper. "I'd suggest each eating off your own plate," she said kindly. Her expression was slightly pleading, the worry in her eyes cleaving a sharp line between her brows. "Trust me on this." She walked away quickly, leaving us to ponder the deeper meaning of two giant slabs of rich cake. We took half of each piece home.

Here was the second and final odd thing: we went back to the restaurant about a month before the Reckoning, and they refused to serve us at all. When we asked why, the owner himself came over and told us our "lifestyle choice" violated his personal belief system. He was a mountain of granite flesh, and looked as though he could eat one of his German Chocolate cakes in its entirety and with little difficulty. His hands dwarfed the reservations book. Dylan, as is his nature, pitched an incendiary fit right in the lobby while I tugged at his sleeve to leave, just go, people are staring. He ranted in the car and then at home, taking his complaint immediately to social media, calling for lawsuits and boycotts. I nervously attempted to downplay it as a singular event, and said the owner was worthy of neither our ongoing business nor even any further attention.

It ended up turning into the worst fight we ever had. He shouted at me about what he called my willingness to participate in my own oppression; I'd never seen such disgust in his eyes, at least not directed at me. I screamed back that I simply wanted to live my life, I was tired of his considering *everything*, including my opinion, a gauntlet thrown down to begin a new battle. He used to love my lack of self-seriousness. Why did he now denigrate those very qualities he said originally attracted him to me?

"Don't you see?" he said later that night in bed, his voice finally soft but shaking. His tears of despair dripped onto my shoulder as we spooned. "Don't you see what's happening, my love?"

I didn't.

Or maybe I did but kept it a secret from myself.

Just Add Water

Last night Betsy made red beans and rice for dinner because she knows it's my favorite. Or it was, in the past. She can't eat much of it, as it plays havoc with her stomach, so for her to make it just for me is extra special. She does little things like that, to be nice.

In her past, Betsy never married. Like cooking, it simply didn't interest her. I know she had five relationships, including a very long-term one with a woman named Rachel, but they weren't together at the time of Reckoning. That's practically the extent of what I know about her past. She doesn't talk much about her old life. When she does, it seems to create a dark cloak that wraps around her for days, so I try to help her focus on the here and now. There's something powerful in sharing your determined optimism; it inspires me as much as her. Our will to live is strong. We try to march resolutely forward in spite of everything, but I know one of us gives up at least once a day. For her it might be harder. She's had so much more imposed on her than I have, from the loss of her career to being forced to wear dresses and makeup and to keep her hair long. It's untamable, and all she can manage is to pull it back into a hideous scrunchie, which makes it appear a strange flowery weed is springing from the back of her head. She's a butch forced to become a femme, and quite frankly she's pretty terrible at it.

   P.S. Her red beans and rice isn't very good. It's from a prepackaged mix, like most of the food they supply us, and always a tad too salty. Even her best dishes are cobbled together from processed ingredients. But it's what we're given.

   Once a week, she is taken by a Good Guy to the barracks commissary to pick up her two boxes of rations. Most of the food is nearing its expiration date by the time it makes its way to us, so the grocery stores were probably planning to toss it; maybe that's how things are done now in the outside world. They don't tell us. Betsy and the other housewives are allowed free choice of three additional items each week, and so it's sweet of her to think of me and use one of those choices for a meal her body will have trouble processing. On those nights, she'll make a pan of cornbread from a just-add-water mix and eat mostly that instead. I don't tell her the dinner is bad. She probably knows.

Shoes and Coffee

Dylan and I had a very ordinary first date, mid-afternoon coffee. The first time I'd met him was in a bar, where he was having a beer with a mutual friend. After he politely turned down my offer to buy him a drink that evening, we kept all of a sudden ending up in the same group activities, like movie nights and cocktail parties. Finally, after a friend's potluck, our fourth meet-up in seven weeks, he asked for my phone number. He was so pokerfaced, I assumed at first it was a joke. He had to ask a third time before I realized it wasn't.

The next day I related this over the phone to our potluck hostess Patti, who said, "Are you kidding? He was terrified. He thinks you're way out of his league." Which shocked me at the time and honestly still does. I know I'm reasonably cute (not hot, not beautiful, but cute), even more so back then, when I had access to things like the gym, hair salons, and shoe stores. I won't put on an air of false modesty and pretend I'm not, because even with the minimal objectivity we afford ourselves, I know I'm not a bad-looking guy. But Dylan was gorgeous.

Is gorgeous. Present tense, please.

So anyway, he called a few days later and asked me to coffee. He suggested a popular chain coffee shop, which surprised me, because I had already made up my mind that he was one of those self-serious, "down with corporate America, everyone support local business" types. This was the sixth time I'd been around him, and I wasn't even sure I'd seen him smile.

So why would I want to date someone like that?

I reiterate: gorgeous.

Even though it was drizzling that afternoon, he waited outside for me as I rounded the corner, which was like bonus point number one. We exchanged awkward hellos, and he held out his right hand as if to shake, but lifted his left arm as though to hug me. We ended up doing a badly choreographed combination of both; it was then I realized his raised left arm was meant to give me shelter under his umbrella. I laughed, and he of course did not.

As he held open the door for me and put a gentle hand on my back (which made me like him quite a bit more), I noticed he was wearing a fabulous pair of tasseled blue loafers, and so I complimented them. He turned slightly crimson and murmured a thank you. It was a blessing that the line was short, because he didn't say a word the whole time we stood there. Instead, he kept his eyes glued to the menu board on the wall behind the counter. Maybe Patti was right, and what I'd mistaken for gravitas was instead some gauche form of shyness. I hoped so. Otherwise, I was in for one glum afternoon.

We got to the register and I ordered a fat-free latte. Dylan ordered a decaf iced tea and ignored my quizzical stare.

"No coffee?" I said as soon as we sat down.

"Naw," he said. "I'm not really a coffee person."

"So if you don't like coffee, why'd we meet here?"

He took a long time pouring in a packet of fake sugar before answering. "Because *you* like coffee. Patti told me the two most important things to you are coffee and shoes. Maybe not in that order." He didn't look *at* me so much as in my general direction.

What was I supposed to say to that? While it was true, it made me sound awfully shallow. After a few seconds of internal debate, I decided owning up to it was probably the best of my options. So I nodded sheepishly and told him Patti didn't lie.

"But," I said, "you do have great shoes. So we have that in common."

"They aren't even mine, I borrowed them from my housemate." Dylan was now completely red-faced. "I wanted to make a good impression."

"Yeah?"

"Yeah." He looked me fully in the eyes for the first time. "You're very. . .I don't even know what to call it. There's kind of a, a lightness about you, and I don't have very much light in my life. My friends and I, we're a pretty serious bunch. I think it would be good for me, to be around that more often."

He was so forthright and sincere, I couldn't help but get a little instant crush on him. Then finally he smiled, a timid and crooked grin, and I was a goner.

Head Count

We haven't had a late night execution in a long time, but I still get scared when the alarms go off.

They set off the alarms this morning at 3:30 and I've been awake more or less since then. It's always frightening when they sound, but the middle of the night is the worst. They don't pull you from sleep so much as slap you upside the head and scream, "Wake up!" It's worse than when I have the bad dreams.

I'm exhausted.

Since they won't tell us what's going on, we never know if there's a genuine emergency or if this is another tactic to keep us off balance.

When the alarms blare, you get out of bed and outside as quickly as possible. You don't want to be late. It is important that you wear your bathrobe.

It's right there in the rule book: "**Do not ever** leave your quarters unless fully dressed. If there is an emergency and the alarm should sound while you are in nightclothes, it is mandatory that you **first** don your robe and tie it securely **before** stepping outside."

What they really mean is: "Do not drive your weak-minded neighbors crazy with desire by exposing your flesh in public." No one uses those words, obviously, but it's what they mean. We are unsexed in every possible way save surgically.

This morning we were up and in our robes and out the door before the Officers and Good Guys made it to our bungalow, one of the advantages of living at the far end of the compound. We stood squinting under the glare of the naked light bulb above our cement stoop. Like everything else, we have no say in this matter; all porch lights go on at dusk and off come the dawn.

Suddenly I realized I didn't have my identification. Betsy typically only needs hers on grocery day or a special occasion, so she hangs her lanyard from the robe hook by the bed. But I am forever setting mine down somewhere after work and forgetting about it.

"Hurry," Betsy said. "Their flashlights are at the end of this row, so you've only got about a minute and a half."

I ran into the house. For such a small place, it now seemed full of endless possibilities of nooks and crannies. I raced through, running my hands over everything with the laser-like efficiency only achieved through panic. I felt the pockets of my trousers hanging in the closet like security patting down a concertgoer before a particularly rowdy show. The flashlight beams were visible through the front window when I remembered dozing off in front of the TV last night. I pulled the cushions off in a fever and saw my ID badge fly into the air and hit the floor. I swooped down and grabbed it, readjusting my robe as I ran through the door. The Good Guys were just approaching from the street.

"ID," one of them said. He looked at our cards, checked two boxes from a list on his clipboard, and said, "Prisoner and Mrs. 34, you can go back inside."

That was all then, just a head count. No crisis, no death.

We went back to bed, and within twenty minutes, Betsy's breathing steadied, deepened. I stared up at the dark, shaking with fear at what might have happened had I not found my badge, fruitlessly willing myself to go back to sleep, and watched the light gradually sneak in and turn the ceiling tiles white.

Doing Nothing Foolish

After they storm-troopered our house, Dylan and I were handcuffed and thrown in the back of an honest-to-goodness paddy wagon. My body was so full of adrenaline I couldn't see clearly, and all I could think through the fog of my confusion was, "I can't believe they still have these." I guess I believed they were some kind of movie prop, a handy myth of second-rate pulp fiction. Didn't they use vans now? Had they already overtaken Hollywood and stolen this one from a studio back lot?

It was, yes, so dramatic, like a movie.

But it was immediately obvious this was no standard arrest; these weren't even police officers. Nobody read us our Miranda rights (or was that only a fictional plot device of the movies, too?). We weren't being arrested, we were being taken.

They deposited us on metal benches facing each other, but as soon as we started driving, I got up and moved over next to Dylan. Walking in a moving vehicle while handcuffed was like stumbling around drunk.

"I didn't think it would happen this soon," he said. "I thought we would have more time to fight."

"Can't we call someone?"

"What are you talking about?" Between the dim light and my jittery vision, I could only see his shape, but there was no mistaking the caustic tone in his voice.

"I just meant. You're an attorney, you should know who to contact."

"Babe. They're not going to give us our one free phone call."

So the police station phone call was a real thing, too?

I didn't know what to say after that. We sat there panting like we'd just finished a marathon. I was suddenly freezing. Every bump in the road created a nuclear-decibel rattle. Dylan leaned toward me. The van stopped suddenly and as I toppled forward his kiss landed on the side of my neck. When I hit the ground he pushed me with his feet, hard, practically kicked me across to my own side of the wagon.

"Get up!" he hissed. "Hurry! Sit down right where they put you."

Then, after a pause: "Don't do anything foolish." I don't know if he said this to me or to himself. The back doors flew open then and they were on us, two men for each of us. They yanked me one in direction and Dylan the other.

A few seconds later I heard him shout my name.

"Yes?" I yelled up into a sky beginning to turn pink.

If he said anything else to me, I didn't hear it. Maybe he was just checking to see if I was safe, or maybe they punched him for yelling.

Speaking Out of Turn

   This morning I was sitting at my desk arranging product files in alphabetical order when a Good Guy ushered in one of the factory workers, Prisoner 79 by his ID. They stood at the counter while Boss A took his time initialing some paperwork, until finally the Good Guy cleared his throat. Boss A finally sighed heavily, as though this were the most inconvenient interruption in the world, and said, "Yes?"

   "Permission to speak, Sir," said the prisoner. He had dark hair and a lankiness I'd have been attracted to under different circumstances.

   "What is it, 79?"

   "There's a problem with the tool that punches the holes in the metal frames," said the worker. "As far as I can tell, we probably just need to replace the handle. The rest seems okay."

   "Get him a requisition form, 34," Boss A said to me. I pulled it from the file and slid it across the counter, careful to not let my hand venture too close to 79's hand.

   "Write down the item you need here," I said, indicating an open space on the form. "We'll fill in the part number for you after the warehouse pulls it."

"Thanks," he said brightly, and his daring scared me a little. Boss A didn't react, so I guess politeness fell in the realm of business-only conversation.

"We'll bring it out in a few minutes," Boss A said. "Is there someone who knows how to fix it?"

"I can do it, Sir," he said. "It's not difficult." He held out the form toward me. I plucked it from his hand carefully with forefinger and thumb and laid it on the counter. His head was bent slightly down, but he raised his eyes to mine and said, quickly and quietly, "Your mother's looking for you."

"What?!" I jerked back so quickly I stumbled and smacked my hip into the corner of my desk. The Good Guy instantly trained his weapon on us like a goon. I raised my hands in surrender, but the worker kept looking right at me.

Boss A was having none of it. "Put your gun down!" he barked to the Good Guy. Then, to the prisoner, "What did you say, 79?"

"I apologize, Sir," 79 said, eyes down at last. "It won't happen again."

"34, do you know this prisoner?" Boss A said, turning to me.

"No, Sir, I don't." Which was the truth. To be safe, I kept my hands up and visible.

"He wasn't in the group I arrived with, but I've seen him in the factory."

"There are rules about talking," he said to the prisoner.

"Yes, Sir, I apologize for talking out of turn. It won't ever happen again, Sir." 79 put his palms together in a gesture of supplication or prayer. "Since he was here in the office, I assumed he was also a Boss."

"79, What did you say to this prisoner?"

"I said, 'Brother, how do you do.' Again, I'm very sorry." He sounded sincere, but when he turned his face slightly away from them, he winked at me.

The Good Guy stood off to the side, staring longingly at his lowered assault rifle, just waiting for the signal to drop the prisoner where he stood.

"Is that what he said?" Boss A asked me.

"I think so, Sir." I lowered my hands very slowly until they rested on either side of the requisition form on the counter, too afraid to meet anyone's eyes. But I was sure I'd heard him right the first time. It seemed wiser not to stir up more questions. "Yes, I'm sure that's what he said."

"Take him back," Boss A said to the guard. Just as they stepped through the door, the

prisoner gave me a quick glance and raised his
eyebrows, but I don't know what it meant.

"M" is For the Many Things You Gave Me...

The last time I visited my mother, we had a fight. It was stupid, not worthy of us, but we fell victim to our mutual stubbornness. Our fight was over, of all things, a chair.

After my father passed away, I made it a point to spend more time with my mother, a few long weekends each year and a longer visit during the summer. Though we all lived in different states, my sister, my younger brother, and I came up with a rotating schedule so she was never without one of us for more than six weeks or so. My older brother lived closest to our childhood home, one town away, and he and his wife assumed the majority of responsibility. We even figured out how to plan major holidays so that every other year the whole extended family could be together; odd years we spent with our spouse's families. It all ran smoothly.

My visit was to last ten days. On day five we went furniture shopping—she had suddenly got what she liked to refer to as one of her "wild ideas" and decided she was sick to death of the arrangement of the living room—and on day six, her purchases were delivered.

One of my mother's quirks is she disliked digging through her purse for tip money while people waited. She refused to look unprepared, and though a good tipper, she especially detested having the contents of her wallet on display so whomever she was tipping could see she had more on hand than she was offering. So it was her custom to step into the next room on the pretext of getting a cold beverage for the deliverymen (see also: electricians and plumbers), and to return with both the drinks and the tip on a serving tray. We had pre-paid the extra $55 to have her old pieces hauled away and so, while she was in the kitchen, I instructed the delivery men to take the sectional, the lamp, the coffee table, and my father's old recliner.

   Mother offered her drinks and generous tip, but not until the two drivers were leaving did she notice the recliner was gone. She insisted they unload it and bring it back. I reminded her she had always hated it; she insisted she did not. We argued with increasing anger while the drivers waited. You could see them praying I won the fight. They'd packed it first in the back of their truck, so its removal necessitated offloading the sectional. I tipped them an extra twenty and apologized for my mother while she glared at me.

   The next day, I tried to help her arrange the new furniture. I kept coming back to the recliner, and how it didn't fit either spatially or stylistically. Our arguing grew more bitter and ridiculous. In the end, I left the stupid thing sitting in the middle of the room and refused to move it another inch.

I should have shut up and let her have her way, but I'm telling you here: while my father was alive, she hated that recliner.

When Dylan called late that afternoon and offhandedly mentioned his car had gone into the shop, I insisted on coming home four days early. He told me it wasn't necessary, but I told my mother the opposite. I gave her only a perfunctory peck on the cheek as I loaded my suitcase into the backseat. And then I drove away. I only waved when I suspected my distance would prevent her from seeing me do so.

Like I said, stupid and beneath us.

But in listing the things I inherited from my mother—things like my hair color, the shape of my nose, and a love of Barbara Stanwyck—one thing I cannot ignore is the ability to dig in my heels at what is sometimes irrational provocation.

I get it from her.

And though I don't get to display this stubborn nature in my current circumstance, I fear it's still there in me.

The Possible Last Time

As I and the others were being herded into the empty car of a train, two days after they had come for Dylan and me, I turned my head to the right, and I think I might have caught a glimpse of him.

He (or someone very similar) was across the track and up from me, and I only caught a one-quarter view of this person's face. It might have been him. The hair curled under his ears the same way Dylan's did, and his chin, from a distance, was similar. They had the same rigid posture. But then the forward momentum of the group pushed me into the car. There wasn't time to call his name.

The Confusing Whatever-It-Is

I'd be lying if I said I don't love Betsy. She's my wife by random assignment, but she's my partner by choice and my one true friend.

I don't know what to call it when Betsy and I do. . .whatever it is we do. Calling it "having sex" feels less emotional than what it is, but it's not really "making love." I guess I could label it "taking comfort." That feels closest to right.

Our whatever-it-is is borne of sadness and pain. It usually begins and ends in tears, and then we can't even look at each other for a couple of hours afterward. Probably I shouldn't let it bother me so much, since it only happens three or maybe four times a year.

If my first marriage (to Dylan) threatened the heterosexual marriages of others, it follows then that my second marriage (to Betsy) somehow stabilizes them. How that works exactly I don't know.

What I do know is, when Betsy got pregnant the first thing I felt was mortification. This was after the monthly Mandatory Conjugation Rule was lifted and the Wardens and Good Guys no longer monitored our intercourse, which made it obvious to all that we'd had sex without the threat of semi-automatic weaponry. Though we lack the legal right to speak to each other, I could read the judgment on the faces of some of the other prisoners, like I was a kind of traitor. Brother Rita, of course, was thrilled when I told him. He assured me this was a great first step toward Changing My Life.

But my life had already changed. I'm a gay man who only has sex with his lesbian wife.

It's not enough.

Tied Hands

I didn't get *officially* scared about what was happening until the day I got fired. We had been assured repeatedly that, though the political climate was changing and the discontent of those with the loudest voices was making waves, the state was not giving in to their demands. There had even been a meeting with the entire staff and union representatives the previous quarter to quell our concerns. We'd already had the same meeting awhile back regarding our Latino coworkers, and none of them was fired.

"No one here is in danger of losing their jobs," we were told, "unless, of course, you break obvious rules." They included everyone in the conversation, even though there were only two of us whose sexuality put us at risk.

So it was a shock when, a few weeks later, I got called into the principal's office and told the school was letting me go, effective right that minute. Two newly installed administrators from the district hovered near the door of his office.

"This isn't my idea," the principal said. He kept his eyes down, concentrating on his fancy granite pen holder. "Please know I would keep you on if it were up to me. I'm so, so sorry."

"But why?" I said, though I already knew the answer. Teachers were being fired across the nation; it was on the news at least twice a week.

"It's out of my control," he said.

"I haven't done anything wrong," I said. The air around me was so thick and hot I could barely draw a breath. "Please."

"I'm so, so sorry," he said again, and raised his hands impotently, as though hoping he could catch hold of a different response in the atmosphere. "These. Tied."

"You'll need to get your things from the room," one of the administrators told me. In her mind it was already *a* classroom and no longer *my* classroom.

I didn't even get to say goodbye to my wonderful class of third graders, my kids, my loves. Instead I was escorted immediately to my classroom and under watchful eyes made to identify each item I packed and justify it as belonging to me and not to the school.

When Dylan walked through the front door a few hours later, I was still sitting on the couch in the darkening living room, my box of useless stuff on my lap, staring at nothing. He dropped his briefcase where he stood and started pacing the room.

The first thing Dylan said was, "They can't do this. We'll fight it in the highest court."

He didn't think to come over and take my hand and hold me against his chest until I burst into tears, several minutes into his rant about the illegalities of my firing. Always the lawyer.

Communiqué

The phone has sat on my desk since day one, but I never realized it works, since it's never rung. Until it did, this morning at 9:30.

I think I might have yelped in surprise; its suddenness scared me. Even Boss A, less emotionally demonstrative, jumped a little. We looked at each other for a second until he, the more quickly composed of us, nodded sharply at me to answer it.

"Hello?" I said. "Production Office." I hated the timidity in my voice.

Silence, for just a moment.

Then, whispered hurriedly: "Your mother is looking for you." *Click*, and the buzz of dial tone.

"Hello?" I said again, more assured this time, already planning things out in my head. I knew what was coming. "Hello, is someone there?"

Sure enough, on cue, Boss A stomped over and grabbed the phone out of my hand.

"Hello!" he shouted, not a question. He looked at the phone; he looked at me. I looked right back at him, into his narrowed eyes, and shrugged.

"That was weird," I said as he handed me the receiver. "I didn't know this phone actually worked." I pushed the button down and then released it, and listened to the hum of technology in my ear before I hung up.

There is still life going on in the world! I've missed it so much; it had somehow ceased to exist for me. If I didn't think about not being a part of the world, the lack of it would hurt less. An action at which I was mostly successful.

"Don't get any ideas, 34," he said.

I shrugged again, gently, passively. "With all due respect, Sir, who would I call?"

"Exactly," he said, the logic of this softening his voice, if not his heart.

"Did they say anything?" he asked, a moment later.

"Nope." I made sure to look him in the eyes again. "Not a word, Sir."

"Get back to work now. We need to get these invoices sorted out within the next hour."

Perhaps he knew how such a small thing like a ringing phone could breathe life back into me, and in that moment took pity on me. Or maybe it scared him, too, even though he didn't hear the message I pretended not to have received.

Still, ten minutes later he made me shake out my blotter.

Twice in less than a month now I've been given the same message. I'm not sure if this message is meant just for me, or for all of us. Is it from my mother, or all our mothers?

Someone, somewhere, is looking.

And someone, somewhere, is making sure I know it.

Something in Something

In the past I laughingly called my encyclopedic treasury of movie factoids useless—because, in truth, what can trivia accomplish, beyond maybe impressing the likeminded and winning party games?—but nowadays I think it has real value. Because there are whole days when the memories of my past life are nebulous, the specifics so hazy I feel like everything that took place before my current reality is some sort of delicious confection I whipped up and ate in my sleep, gone by morning.

What grounds me in reality is being able to remember facts like these:

Q: What color is Norma Shearer's nail polish in *The Women*?

A: Jungle Red!

Q: In *Vertigo*, what's the name of the painting with which Madeline is obsessed?

A: *Portrait of Carlotta*.

Trivial, yes, but solid facts I learned when I had the freedom to watch whatever I wanted, whenever I wanted, over and over, pausing to copy a grand gesture, rewinding until I memorized a great line of dialogue. Proof I had a life. Proof the silly little pleasures of said life added up to great joy.

Three nights ago, I awoke to find I couldn't remember the name of Margo Channing's Broadway play in *All About Eve*. Not the one Lloyd writes later, which Eve steals from her, but the one Margo is in at the beginning, when Karen brings Eve backstage.

No matter how gently I told myself to forget about it and go back to sleep, I laid awake grinding my teeth. I can recite almost every line of dialogue in that movie, but even as I mouthed them in the dark, the name of the play wouldn't come. It's called *Something in Something*; I'm lucky I remember that much.

I don't care how ridiculous it might seem to someone else, to me it matters.

Attempted Nurture

After he says his prayers for me, Brother Rita always asks me to tell him about everything that's transpired since our last meeting. There's usually not much to tell. What could possibly be new when every day (and every week, every month, every year) is exactly the same?

Ah, but now everything might be different. Someone might be looking for me. There is so much I could tell him. But I don't, of course.

I honestly don't dislike Brother Rita. He's kindhearted and appears to sympathize with my plight. But his job is to convince me to become straight, like he is. And while I know his past means he will never fully be "one of them," it doesn't mean I trust him. Who's to say he isn't looking for that nugget of information he can barter to gain credibility and power in the world we occupy?

So last night when he asked me what was on my mind, I shook my head and stared at the floor.

"What is it, 34?" he said. He reached a hand out toward my shoulder, but immediately let it drop to his lap. His eyes flicked automatically toward the ceiling, the hidden camera.

"Nothing," I said. "I guess I'm just missing my family tonight. It's been so long since I've seen my, my brothers and my sister." I intended to say "my mother," but this plan suddenly felt dangerous. For the first time, it occurred to me that perhaps they weren't only watching us at the front desk, but listening, too.

"Yes, it must be hard." Brother Rita pursed his lips. "I remember when I lost my family. But once I turned my life around, they welcomed me back with all the love in their hearts!" His eyes misted over with the kind of glorious tears that would have made Loretta Young proud.

"But I don't have that choice," I said, and the truth of it ripped up my insides. "It doesn't matter if I change or not, I'll still be in here and they'll be out there."

"True, you may not be reunited with them in *this* life, but that doesn't mean you won't all meet again." And Brother Rita was off, reading me passages from his thick, well-thumbed Bible. I never got a chance to work the conversation back to my mother.

I wanted to see his eyes when I said I hoped my mother was looking for me. Just one diva gasp from him and I'd know if she was.

Instead, I asked him, as he dropped me off at my front door, if he knew the name of Margo Channing's play.

The play was called *Aged in Wood*. He knew it without pausing to think. What a queen. I thanked him sincerely, with tears in my own eyes this time.

Another thing I realized, sitting in Brother Rita's office: I have no idea, after six silent years, if my mother is still alive.

Proof by Example

Two years ago today Betsy had the baby.

When we told the Administrator of our barracks Betsy was pregnant, he was delighted. We were the first couple to conceive! We'd be an example to the others! Though still addressed by our number, for the first time they seemed to forget we were prisoners; suddenly we weren't two people forced together by law, but an actual, honest-to-goodness married couple. We were proof this whole system they'd put into play really worked.

For the next eight months, it was doctor appointments and a near-constant stream of official visits to check her progress and to discuss proper nutrition. We ate like royalty, always an extra box of Grade A rations. Three days a week we were allowed to take an evening walk, just the two of us, around the central hub of housing, to assure Betsy got exercise.

We even got books, the ultimate taboo. Books about what was happening in Betsy's body and the birthing process and aftercare. Both of us devoured every word of them several times. It felt so amazing to read books again!

Our questions about cribs and strollers and changing tables were shrugged off with "Don't you worry" or "We've got all that taken care of," but the tone of their answers never implied we wouldn't need them.

It honestly never occurred to us we wouldn't be allowed to keep our baby.

When Betsy went into labor, I was notified, though not allowed to leave work. I chalked it up to one more in the long line of antiquated values they espoused; after all, in olden days, men weren't there in the delivery room, either. Three hours later I was informed she'd had the baby and I could go home early. They even gave me the rest of the week off. I felt I was owed at least the ceremonial cigar, but there wasn't so much as a handshake. But none of it mattered by comparison to knowing I had a child. I walked home as quickly as I could; no running, that's one of the strictest rules. Good Guys are trained to assume "Someone running is someone escaping."

Betsy was half-sitting up in bed when I arrived, an elderly nurse in a hard-backed chair a few feet away. She greeted me not with congratulations, but a list of instructions on how to care for Betsy over the next few days. Very businesslike, no warmth penetrating from behind those silver eyeglasses. As she explained my duties to me, she gathered up all the baby books we'd been allowed to read and stuffed them in a satchel.

"Wait," I said, once I realized she was preparing to leave. "What about the baby?"

"What about it?" She pulled her glasses down and let them hang from their pearl chain.

"Well, where is she? Is she still in the hospital? When can she come home?"

The nurse was very short, but she straightened her spine so forcefully she seemed to grow a foot taller. She reared back her head to look up at me, and I knew what was coming before she opened her twisted mouth.

"You aren't serious?" Her unadulterated disgust was fearsome. "She's been mercifully adopted by a *real* couple. Do you think we'd let an innocent baby be raised by. . .people like you?!" She shooed me away from the door with her book bag, as though to touch me with her own bare hands would scald them, and ran out.

"They didn't even let me hold her," Betsy said thickly from the bed. "They shot me up with something as soon as she was born. I woke up here." I sat on the edge of the bed and held her limp hand. She was so out of it she couldn't even cry, just whimper like a little kid.

"Honey," I said, which was probably the first term of endearment that ever passed between us. We've always only called each other by our names. "Honey, I'm so sorry."

She looked up at me with eyes that didn't quite move in unison.

"I heard her cry," she said, licking her lips with a lazy tongue. "She's healthy, she's got a good set of lungs."

"That's wonderful," I said, trying to smile.

"No," said Betsy. She closed her eyes. "I'd rather she were dead than be raised by those kinds of people. I would have murdered her myself, if they had put her in my arms."

Perhaps it was the drugs talking and she has no recollection of the conversation, because she's never mentioned killing the baby again. But these past two years, something has gone out of her. She's still as strong as she ever was, keeps going through even the most troubling times, but I wonder why she bothers. Living seems like a chore to her now.

Differences

I like it that Dylan and I confused people. We were such a Least Likely couple.

"You have, like, nothing in common," Bernadette said to me over drinks the night after I introduced them. "Don't get me wrong, I liked him. But boyfriend needs to learn to speak up."

"He's shy," I said. Suddenly I felt very protective of him, which was a nice feeling. I hadn't liked someone enough to care what others thought about them in a very long time. Too often I let the catty remarks of my friends make me reconsider a prospective partner through their eyes; and once I looked at his differences through that prism, I lost interest quickly. But I felt Dylan deserved to be explained and defended.

"It took me about half an hour to realize his silence didn't mean he was judging me." Bernadette knocked back the rest of her wine. "He wasn't, was he? Judging me?"

"No," I said, winking at her, "that was me."

"Anyway. He's very nice, he's very cute, and he clearly makes you very happy."

"That's a whole lot of very."

"So of course I approve," she said, waggling her fingers at the waiter for a second round. "But honey. Seriously. What do you guys have in common? No offense. He appears to have no sense of humor, he doesn't drink coffee, and he hates musicals." She ticked them off on her fingers.

"He's also the smartest person I've ever met," I said, half rising from my chair in excitement and holding my own fingers up in response, "he's genuinely interested in what I have to say, and he loves my cooking. Oh! And he loves movies."

"And we all know that's the deal breaker for you." Bern raised her new drink in a toast. "Teach him to worship at the Church of Sondheim and you'll have a match made in heaven."

But Dylan never learned to appreciate Sondheim. Or any musicals, for that matter. But he loved that I loved them, and he listened patiently when I tried to tell him why. He didn't mind that I played original cast recordings in the car. My friends never saw that side of him, that kindness, the visible love in his eyes when I talked about things which were important to me, even if he personally had no interest in them.

His best friend Chad, I later learned, had the same kind of conversation with Dylan about me. The ticking off of reasons on the fingers: I was someone who didn't understand politics deeply enough; who trah-lah-lahed my way through life; who was sweet and, yes, even smart, but not to be taken seriously. "Come *on*," said Chad. "He's got a show tune for every occasion!" (All true, except the "not to be taken seriously" part. I won Dylan, didn't I? I'd take *that* seriously if I were you, Chad.)

But we knew what we had, and never felt compelled to explain it to others. On both sides, families and friends came to like and accept us, but no one ever "got" us. You could see their confusion in the way they crinkled their noses when they looked at us together.

Every time we saw them do that, we would hook our index fingers together and shake, our secret little signal that meant, "We just got stronger."

Alarms

I wish they'd stop with the late night alarms. How do they expect us to give one hundred percent at work when they blast us out of bed early? Don't they know working on an assembly line takes concentration? The poor guys out in the factory, I don't know how they function on nights when we've had a head count.

I suppose I should be thankful they waited until a little before five this morning. It means we got only an hour-plus less sleep than usual.

This seems to be happening more and more often lately. I don't know what they're looking for, but I wish they'd find it already and leave us alone.

Vandalism

As we walked in formation to work yesterday morning, the line suddenly got twisted and haphazard as each prisoner went by the front entrance of the barracks and saw it. People slowed their step, or stopped altogether, resulting in unavoidable congestion. In the confusion, somebody ran a hand quickly down my backside; it wasn't necessarily sexual, and maybe was simply an accident, but the contact felt glorious.

Painted across the entrance gate, in huge block letters, was the message, "YOUR MOTHER IS LOOKING FOR YOU!!!" Three exclamation points, that's not an editorial change on my part. You could hear the murmurs of "Mother" ripple through the crowd as everyone tried to figure out what was happening.

An Officer yelled at us to shut up and the nearest Good Guys instinctively all drew their weapons. No one spoke after that, but we prisoners openly looked at each other's faces for answers, questioning with our eyes: who knew something, who could tell us what was going on. But each pair of eyes I met was as blank and confused as mine. I craned my neck, looking for the prisoner who spoke to me in the office that day, but didn't see him. He could be dead by now for all I know, killed for his insurgent act of speaking out of turn.

About a third of the prisoners were pulled off factory duty for the day and made to paint over the graffiti. If nothing else came of it, for the first time we have an actual painted gate instead of those untreated slats of wood the color of dirt. Our gate is a dark olive green, very military.

But now everyone who looks at it knows what's underneath.

Coffee Ice Cream

All this Mother stuff the last few months has me constantly thinking about my mom. While on the one hand these messages offer a reason to hope maybe someone really is trying to find us, on the other it stirs up so much memory and pain.

I wish we weren't cut off from the outside world. How I would love to be able to go online and just read the news. I used to hate the news, it was like a giant jolt of reality harshing my feel-good buzz. But I'd gladly read it now, I'd eat it up like my favorite dessert. (Which is coffee ice cream, if you're looking for the perfect gift idea, ha-ha.)

Anyway. I guess nothing much to write this afternoon. It's the kind of day where I'm not depressed, but I know if I let my mind go there I will be. My ability to remain upbeat has always been my lion's mane. So I guess I'll take my leave and get distracted by doing my actual job.

There's only so much one can say about coffee ice cream, after all. Though I could tell the story about the time I ate too much too close to bedtime and bounced off the walls half the night. Actually, that *is* the whole story. I ate too much coffee ice cream and bounced off the walls half the night.

The end.

Hi.

Don't be scared. I knew someday I'd get my courage up to answer you. You don't know me, but you've wondered about me a few times. I'm the guy that's on the other end of your computer, the one you send your reports to. The guy you refer to as You.

I can tell you what's happening on the outside. . .

An Introduction

It's been over two weeks since you've written anything. I get your reports every Tuesday and Friday, so I know you're still at work. Your initials are always there at the top of the page, "grf." I have no idea what they stand for, so in my head I always pronounce your name Griff.

My name is Jerry Campbell. My job is to keep track of inventory from all the different factories, so every day I monitor the reports that come in. Every factory has a person who does your job, and I take all the information and put it on a massive spreadsheet. It's not very glamorous, ha-ha. The person reading your thoughts is not very important, in the grand scheme of things.

I like your reports the best because of the things you write. You're the only person who does that. I guess the others never thought of it, or maybe you're the only brave one.

All the reports are staggered, meaning people write them at different days and times. My office machinery is very antiquated, more than one report at a time screws everything up. You used to write yours while I was at lunch, but one Friday I got caught up with a very long phone call. Imagine my surprise when all of a sudden my computer screen started filling up with these words. And then just about the time I realized what I was reading, they started deleting themselves! The next Tuesday I stuck around, pretending I was busy with something and couldn't go to lunch on time, and I read the whole thing before it disappeared. You type fast, so I have to be on my toes and read quickly or I'll miss the end. I finally switched lunch times with a coworker so I could read your thoughts every time.

Anyway, I wanted to introduce myself, so you wouldn't be afraid to write anymore, if that is the reason you've stopped.

I promise I haven't told anyone about what you do, not even my wife.

An Apology

Dear Griff,

I've given you another week, figuring maybe you needed some time to process that someone actually is on the other end of your computer, but still no word from you.

Please keep writing. Your words have moved me. A lot. I didn't realize everything that was going on with you people. I mean, I knew they dissolved all the gay marriages and then outlawed homosexuality, and to be honest right up front, I support those laws. Just so you know. But not everyone who is against your lifestyle choices is in favor of what the new government has done to you.

Also, please know that your writing really has opened my eyes to the way you've been treated. I had no idea. Well, that's not totally true. I knew they took everyone away, and I knew that the factory workers were all homosexuals, but I didn't know how much you were abused at first and put in camps, and I really didn't know they made all of you folks marry each other. That seems cruel, and is as much a desecration of the sanctity of marriage as what we were fighting against in the first place.

I'm truly sorry this has happened to you.

I hope you will write more soon.

I'm trying to make this really short so you can read it in the ten minutes you have. After all this time, I know exactly when those ten minutes are, so don't worry, I will never write anything at a different time of day and cause you to get in trouble. Just delete this when you're done reading.

Jerry

Trust

Dear Griff,

Okay, I'm taking your silence as a lack of trust. I respect that. If I were you, I might not trust me, either. After all that's happened, who can blame you for thinking this stranger writing to you might be a bad guy? You even said that once.

So I'm going to give you reasons to trust me, alright?

First off, if I were bad, I would have turned in you long ago. I'm just an office drone, so if I wanted to get ahead unethically, I would have done it by now. Many gays have been caught living among us, pretending to be straight. Turning them in to the authorities can be financially beneficial and leveraged for business promotions, especially after the government and the corporations merged and became the same entity.

Second, you told me once that you used aliases, but then you made one mistake. Do you remember? Did you catch it at the time and instantly regret it? You wrote the name of your piano teacher, Mrs. Sharp, and then wrote "I swear" right after it. If you were making up an alias, you would never have pointed out the humor of her name. So there is another way I could have tracked you down, if I'd wanted to.

Third and most obvious of all, I'm going to naturally assume the "grf" at the beginning of every report is really your initials. Why would you fudge those? I don't think your Boss A would let you get away with that. All I'd need to do is ask someone, "Who writes the South Carolina reports?"

There, I just told you where you are, South Carolina. That could get me in trouble, too. Betsy was close, guessing Georgia.

Quid Pro Quo

Dear Griff,

I first wrote to you over a whole month ago, and you've yet to respond. You weren't kidding when you said you were stubborn, were you, LOL? Well, guess what, I'm pretty stubborn myself.

So here's what I'm proposing to do. I'm going to keep writing at the same time, let's say once a week. Returning the favor, so to speak.

Maybe someday you'll realize you can actually trust me and write me in return. Feel free to interrupt at any time, like I did to you.

Your friend,

Jerry

The Facts of (Jerry's) Life

Hello Griff,

I've spent the last week trying to decide what to write about. You always have so much on your mind to say, more than you can usually fit into a ten-minute slot, it seems to me. How do you decide what your topic is each day? Or do you just write what's on your mind? It's been so distracting for me, worrying about it, that last night my wife even said, "What's going on with you lately? You seem like you're not here." I told her it was work stuff, which is true, or at least true enough so I can feel like I didn't lie to her.

This morning the obvious answer dawned on me. You've told me so much of your life story, even though you didn't know I was there, so I figured I can tell you about mine.

I am 38 years old, which I think is around your age, if I'm not mistaken. My guess is you're 38 to 42, am I close?

I was born in Oklahoma, but have lived most of my life in Ohio, starting from college onward. It's this dumb joke of mine, I call myself Double-O, because I've only lived in those two states and they both begin with the letter O. Don't worry if you didn't laugh, you aren't alone, nobody thinks it's funny but me.

Today I live outside Cincinnati. I am married and have two children.

So I guess that's enough for today. It's taken me about five minutes to write this, so I'll stop now so you have a chance to read it and delete.

Jerry

Needs of the State

Dear Griff,

I guess today I will tell you about my family, since I know something about yours. My wife's name is Ellen. That's not an alias, by the way, LOL. For years she worked in Accounts Payable for a large company, but once the schools got so bad, she quit her job and started homeschooling our children. It was cheaper to live on my single paycheck than it was for her to keep working and pay for our kids to go to a private school. Had she made more money than me at her job, right now I'd be a stay-at-home dad and homeschooler and wouldn't be writing this!

It's been a real sacrifice, though, living on one paycheck, especially since the sanctions from so many other countries that refuse to support our government made our economy tank and I took a substantial cut in pay. But the whole nation's going through it, so I try not to complain too hard. We are standing together as a nation and weathering the financial storm.

The greatest thing to come out of the lack of imported goods has been the increase of new jobs in the US. More people are working! Again, it's because so many other governments refuse to allow our corporations to set up factories in their countries, but it has had a good effect on our job force. No one makes as much now, and the dollar is worth less than it used to be, but it has shown us how to be thrifty and careful. I can't speak for everyone, of course, but the people in my town have become adept at getting by on less. We are thankful for what we do have, and try not to demand more than the government has to offer. And the need for our own homeland fruits and vegetables and grains has been a blessing for farmers!

Indeed, the lack of imports and exports is another reason all of you in the factories deserve our thanks. Take the factory where you work, for instance. Without the computer monitors you guys manufacture, we wouldn't have much in the way of technology. We only have what we make ourselves now. True, what we do have is behind the cutting edge of a few other countries, but it's enough. My printer may be old and outdated so I can only print one report at a time, but it's sufficient to get me by.

"Enough" has become a way of life, the new American motto for many of us. In some ways, this economic crisis has been a real wakeup call about our own greed and consumption. Last week in the state of the union address, the President reminded us that we are the new pioneers, re-forging the traditional American value of self-sufficiency.

Okay, I've gone on way too long. I hope you have time to read all this before your Boss A comes back. This didn't turn out to be much about my family at all, sorry about that.

Your friend,

Jerry

Left-Handed

Dear Griff,

I feel a good part of the reason behind your silence is probably my early statement that I do not approve of your homosexual lifestyle. Maybe I mentioned it too soon and got us off on the wrong foot, but since it's been brought out into the open, I may as well address it sooner than later. While I won't apologize for my beliefs, I will say I'm sorry if my statement hurt you. I'm not a hateful person, I just believe in what I believe to be wrong and right.

Here is how I look at it: I'm right-handed. Most people are. Now, imagine all the left-handed people suddenly start marching and protesting and tell all of us righties that we have to use our left hands to make everyone "equal" under the law. For a right-handed person, being forced to be a leftie is "unnatural." It doesn't mean I hate left-handed people, but I don't want it forced on me. Does that make sense?

I feel that way about homosexuality. I don't care what you do in the privacy of your home, it does not affect my life. At all. But when you bring it out into the streets and I'm forced to accept it and explain it to my children, then we've got a problem. How do I explain to my eight-year-old daughter why there are two men kissing in front of her?

Hopefully, explaining where I stand hasn't made our relationship worse, but I felt it was important to talk about the proverbial elephant in the room.

I don't hate you or anyone else. To me, hate is a grave sin. I have had many friends over the years who don't share my beliefs, or my background, or who don't have any externals in common with me other than being human beings.

Your friend,

Jerry

Rumors

I know it's been weeks since I've written. There's been very little time. This one will probably have to be short. Everything in the world feels crazy right now.

Things are happening that I don't feel I can talk about with you. It's not that I don't trust you, especially since I've asked you to trust me, but at this stage, passing along certain information seems dangerous for all of us.

Suffice it to say, there's so many acts of insurrection going on, not to mention global threats, and hints and rumors of war, you're probably better off than me right now, tucked away where no one can get to you. The rebels have no problem bombing any government corporation they can, but since they're doing it at least partly as protest for you guys being locked up, it would be counterproductive for them to bomb the factories, don't you think? I'm pretty sure you're all safe.

I will write when I can. Even with the mayhem and all my putting out fires (once literally, when there was a Molotov cocktail thrown through our doorway!), I am still at my desk every day and here at the same time if you want to write back.

Jerry

A Second Apology

Dear Griff,

I feel I owe you an apology for that last letter. Because of events that were going on I was kind of wigging out, which is not my usual disposition.

Believe me when I say things are not as bad as I made them out to be. Yes, there is a lot of stuff happening in our country and the world, I'm not gonna lie. But I probably made it sound like World War III was erupting and that's not true. If I were to try and come up with a better description, it's closer to Civil War. But that's not really accurate, either, since so many people left when the government changed. There was such a mass migration to Canada that it wouldn't surprise me to learn their population doubled. Some people went south, but as you might imagine, the Mexican government wasn't too keen on accepting our emigrants, when we'd just shipped theirs back to them rather forcibly. So the non-Mexicans were refused crossing.

Anyway, all of this is information you don't have to worry about. Like I said before, I feel you are safe. No one wants to bomb the people whose imprisonment practically started this whole thing, after all.

Jerry

More Rumors

Dear Griff,

I wish I could help with the "Your mother is trying to find you" thing, but information is very limited. Slowly but surely, the government has restored the internet, but it is closely monitored by the Department of Online Information and they selectively decide what sites we are allowed to see. I've tried using the one legal US search engine to indirectly see if I can find anything, but nothing comes up. I hesitate to actually enter that phrase into the computer. I don't want to send any red flags. I have a family to protect, after all.

To my knowledge, our communication here is not monitored, as it is in theory just the transmitting of work-related numbers from one person to another. But in our case theory is not quite fact. I think we're safe, though. Surely someone would have questioned me about it by now, if they were watching.

I just wanted to let you know I did try to answer your questions. I have no idea what the messages mean, because it's hard with select news coverage to know what's real and what's rumor. There is supposedly a huge movement from the emigrants to Canada to free the camps, but I have no idea where the rumor originated or if it's true.

Sorry I couldn't be more help. I honestly would tell you if I knew something, so it might give you some peace of mind.

Your friend,

Jerry

The Reason for the Season

Dear Griff,

Since you work in the office and can see the calendar, I know you know that Christmas is approaching. Since our office will be closed for over a week for the holidays, we are all extremely busy here. Just in case I don't have time to write you, I wanted to say Merry Christmas now while I had the chance. I understand it is difficult for you, but I hope you will take the meaning of the day to heart and let that give you some comfort.

Merry Christmas. That may sound like an empty sentiment, but I wanted to say it anyway. I do only wish you the best and all happiness you can find.

Your friend,

Jerry

The Safety of an Absent Reader

My Dearest Double-O,

This will be deleted by the time you get back from your holidays. It's Christmas Day; I'm working. Enjoy your turkey!

You're right about a few things, Jerry, especially my silence.

No, I *don't* trust you, not even after you gave me a list of reasons why I should. That's *exactly* what someone trying to instill trust would say.

If you think I'm better off locked away here as a prisoner than you are out in the free world, then I don't even know what to say to you. I would give *anything* to be free! Back when my rights were being eroded, I thought the world was a pretty bleak place, but it was paradise compared to what I have now.

You've instilled a new and different degree of fear in me, Jerry, the fear of goodhearted people who can't recognize cruelty where it exists, because it doesn't contradict their belief system. But as long as you project onto my silence whatever you think it means, maybe you'll continue to tell me about a world existing outside this gate and the razor-wired walls that contain me. So there's the interruption to your ramblings I've been too afraid to make.

Oh, except I will add one more thing. How do you explain to your eight-year-old daughter why two men are kissing?

Try this: "Most boys like girls and most girls like boys. But some boys like boys and some girls like girls." Every single child I've said this to had the same reaction. "Oh," they said, "okay." And then they go on to the next thing.

There you go, crisis averted. You're welcome.

Your "left-handed" pal, grf

A New Year

Dear Griff,

The beginning of a new year always gives me cause to reflect and look at what I've accomplished and left undone. This year is especially meaningful because I've not only made a new friend, but I have come to the end of the year a stronger man.

Surviving the persecution I've undergone in the last year has, I hope, made me a better person. Just because we are now a conservative nation doesn't mean that everyone who didn't flee the country is on our side, or is a Christian. I am harassed on a daily basis, sometimes subtly but sometimes openly, by liberals. It's so unfair, and it makes me feel like I understand you better.

But how I look at it is this: I have held my head up in the face of adversity, and part of that strength has come from reading about you doing the same. Like I've said many times, your words affect me. I've learned from you.

So now I'm reminding you to keep your head up, too. You may not believe you will be rewarded for your suffering, but I believe it strongly enough for both of us.

I will not say "Happy New Year," as that seems thoughtless and mean-spirited. But I will say, "Hang in there, buddy."

Your friend,

Jerry

Love the Sinner

Dear Griff,

Last Sunday at church the sermon was about love. The pastor mentioned "Love the sinner, hate his sin" and I thought of you. Have you ever heard that phrase before?

Jerry, stop. Just stop it. I know your intentions are good, but today is not the day. I don't want to hear about how you're just like me. You are nothing like me.

Because everything is different now.

Brother Rita is dead.

What Was Hidden in Plain Sight

    Last Monday night at 10:30, the day after you thought of me in church, the alarms sounded. All the lights in the barracks came on, giant overheads so bright you couldn't look directly at them, the entire place brilliant as daylight. We took our places on the porch and waited, and waited, and waited, but no one came to check our IDs.

    Finally, over the loudspeakers came the announcement that we were all to walk to the center of the barracks, the same place where Betsy and I had first met. When we got there a group of Good Guys surrounded all of us, guns at the ready. One of the Officers told us to stay put and not move.

    Groups of Officers ran from bungalow to bungalow. You could hear them rampaging through the apartments, overturning furniture. Betsy held my hand, and this time I don't think she was offering strength but searching for it. Nobody dared speak.

    After about fifteen minutes a shout rose up from one of the bungalows a couple of streets over. They'd found whatever it was they were looking for. A noisy group of them began marching back toward us, flanking whatever they had confiscated from the house. When I noticed their rubber gloves I began to shiver so hard Betsy threw an arm around my shoulders to steady me. When they got to the center, the tight circle opened and there in the middle of them stood Brother Rita and some other prisoner, a man younger than me who was in my original group but whose name I don't remember. They were beaten, crying, naked. Their bloodied faces reminded me of Frederick's just before he was killed at the hangar, but these injuries were much more severe, and I knew they'd felt the butt of more than one rifle.

It's been so long since we've had a killing at the barracks, I forgot the gallows was still there. If you don't have reason to look up, you wouldn't notice it unobtrusively built onto the side of the two-story Administration Building, hiding in plain sight.

The two nooses were quickly lowered. I couldn't stop staring at Brother Rita, no matter how badly I wanted to turn away. I couldn't wrap my brain around his nakedness. He begged for mercy, crying so hard he fell to the ground. They simply lowered his noose further.

"This," said the Administrator, patrolling the area before us with his megaphone, "is why you're all here. This is not only a sin, it is criminal activity. And criminal activity will not be tolerated!" He pointed at the two prisoners, Brother Rita on the ground and the other man looking straight ahead blankly, either being brave or so terrified and cold he'd gone numb. "Look at what their sin has gotten them."

   We stood silent, bundled against the cold in our nightwear and our robes. The only sound was Brother Rita's frantic screams of apology and prayer. At the Administrator's gesture, the Officers on either side of the gallows pulled the ropes. I looked down at the dirt at last, and a couple of seconds later Brother Rita's wailing stopped.

The Fate Worse Than Death

I've had a few days now to try and make sense of what's happened. Not just to Brother Rita, but to me, too. I appreciate that you haven't written, Jerry, and have afforded me the privacy in which to grieve. There's been so much to consider here, more than might be apparent from the outside.

What has affected me most profoundly on the night Brother Rita was killed is his nudity. In that moment, despite his crying and bleeding, and in the most nonsexual situation imaginable, all I could think about was his nakedness. It's true. His body was beautiful. Who knew he was hiding such magnificence under those silly cardigans and corduroys? I *ached* at the sight of his naked body. His is the first I've seen since Dylan's (unless you count the showers in the camp, but with all the guns on us, I made sure never to let my eyes roam), and I wanted him more than I've wanted anyone in years, maybe ever.

So if you think my sexuality and my life is a *choice* I made, you'd better reconsider your notion of choice. This is the kind of lust one would experience as a teenager when out of the blue in some dumb movie there would be a flash of nudity. It didn't matter what else was happening, because in your silly virgin brain, all you saw was flesh. Who wouldn't be ashamed to realize that, in the midst of observing such suffering as Brother Rita's, one couldn't rise above their basest desire? A desire so ingrained in me, no circumstance can change it or turn it off. I looked away when they pulled the ropes because I didn't want to see him die, but I also looked away so that when my brain replayed his nakedness later, as I knew it would, I didn't have to picture a corpse. How sad is that?

The thought I kept batting away while he cried and appealed to his captors' nonexistent humanity was that all this time he'd secretly been having sex, but it wasn't with me. He didn't choose me. While he agonized in his last minutes of life, the only things I felt were desire and self-pity.

And I don't know what that says about me.

If I'd known Brother Rita was willing, I would have set about trying to seduce him a long time ago. What else that means is, I would have been killed right along with him the other night.

And I know this as surely as I know my name: it would have totally been worth it.

That's the part gnawing at me, you see. I've been cowed and abused all these years because I have wanted so badly to live. It didn't matter the circumstance, I put up with everything in order to stay alive, because I feared death so strongly.

But I don't feel that way anymore. I don't think I fear death now. No longer fearing death should feel transcendent, shouldn't it, like achieving a state of grace. But this doesn't feel that way. Instead it feels like I've finally been broken.

The Four of Spades

One day a few months ago, Betsy went to the commissary for our rations, and there in one of the food boxes was a deck of playing cards. They told her it was a new addition to the Humane Laws, something fun for couples to do together. It turned out to be a pretty great idea, really, a nice alternative to the sometimes silly TV programming.

The cards were cheap and flimsy, though, and within a few weeks one of them got ruined. The four of spades got caught in the metal piping at the edge of the dinner table and ripped right in two when I tried to unstick it. We taped it back together, and continued playing our games of Rummy and Go Fish. But we always knew when the other had that card. It went from being a source of amusement ("I know what card *you've* got") to affecting the strategy of play. We began to actually play to win, and sometimes we fought about the outcome. That ripped card became emblematic of everything that was untenable about our situation, and eventually we started playing less and less. Now we rarely play at all.

Wow. What am I thinking? Is this what I'm reduced to writing about? I can't stand it.

The Only Feeling Left Alive

For the last couple of Tuesdays and Fridays, as Boss A steps into Boss B's office, I've tried to decide what to write about for my unstructured ten minutes, and each time I've drawn a complete blank.

I don't know if I have anything left to say. Anything I have left to say at this point is trivial. In the context of the life I am living, writing about minutiae seems stupid. The desire to communicate, to get my words out, has faded, until now I'm just numb.

Every day is the same.

This is my life.

What more is there to say about it?

When I do allow my numbness to subside, the only emotion my body affords me now is rage. I don't even know at whom it's directed anymore. The government? The Bosses? God?

Is it directed at you, Jerry?

Or is my rage directed at me for trying so hard to see the good in the world that I couldn't accept what was happening around me? What Dylan's best friend Chad said about me was right. I trah-lah-lahed my way through life. Even as a prisoner, I tried to do the same thing. Buck up, soldier on, look for the small blessings that allow me to not want to kill myself and everyone around me.

You told me you don't hate me, Jerry, and you expressed sorrow and sympathy for what they did to us. But where were you when these plans were taking shape? You knew there was a crusade against us. Even if you disagreed with my "lifestyle," as you insist on calling it, you knew whatever was in store for us was wrong. Did you say anything? Did you fight for the dignity of your fellow man?

No, you sat idly by. And that's what I did, too.

We both let it happen.

I don't think I'm going to write anymore. Knowing someone is actually reading this makes me too self-conscious.

Not knowing for sure allowed me a certain freedom of expression I no longer have. Instead I write about playing cards, and worry that in saying that little, I'm giving away my soul to be read by someone I don't even respect.

Please don't write to me again, Jerry.

On either side of the fence, we have nothing more to say.

Forewarning

Dear Griff,

PLEASE READ THIS! DON'T DELETE WITHOUT READING!

I have tried to honor your wishes and leave you alone. Every Tuesday and Friday for the last four months I've seen your initials at the top of the report and my heart aches with wanting to say something, give you some apology or comfort. And I haven't.

But I really need you read this. I know you are there today, on the other end of the computer, because I see you've already started your report.

My information is limited, but I can tell you this. "Your mother is looking for you," which started as a rebellion, spawned a movement which has spawned a rebel army and a war, part of it civil and part of it international.

We are at war. Our nation is under attack from inside and out, an actual war, right here on our home turf. We get real news reports now, warnings from the government, what's left of it. The President has gone into hiding, and I'm not even sure who is in charge at this stage. The bombings and killings are racking up massive casualties. Many of the larger cities have been taken back already. My small town is safe, at least right now, but I never know what I'm going to find when I drive into Cincinnati each morning. I'm at work today, but for all I know my building may not be standing tomorrow.

At least three factories have been liberated. The government has begun moving all the prisoners to other locations. I don't know where. All I can think is, at least they aren't killing you guys, but I can't swear that in time they won't. They seem unwilling to give you all up. It's like a matter of principle.

I don't know what's going to happen, so please be careful.

The End

Dear Jerry,

As I sit at my desk writing this, there is a dead body on the floor maybe three feet away from me. It is several hours earlier than I usually write and it is a Monday, the wrong day of the week even.

For once there is no time constraint. When I am done, I won't hit delete.

This morning the alarms went off at 7:48, just as the men were about to leave for work. Betsy and I stepped outside and put our shoes on while standing on the porch. A late spring morning, already bright and sunny, but colder than I expected. I just told Betsy I should go grab a jacket when a Good Guy ran up to our porch and told us to come with him immediately. Since I no longer care if they shoot me, I boldly asked him what was happening, but he ignored me and hurried us along, pointing his gun for emphasis toward the center of the barracks.

We didn't march politely and slowly as we've always been instructed. He kept telling us to move faster, pick up the pace. For the first time in years, we were allowed to run. It felt weird, like my legs couldn't quite remember what they were supposed to do. I almost fell twice, so out of shape it's embarrassing.

When we arrived in the barracks center, everyone was there, the Administrator and the Officers and the Good Guys, the entire staff of around-the-clock crews and prisoners all at the same time, almost too many of us to fit. It takes a lot of people to run a barracks, I had no idea how many.

I had told Betsy about the message you sent last week, so we already suspected we were being moved, even before the open-bed trucks showed up. The air was filled with incessant beeping as they backed in and enclosed us, as though they were a corral of covered wagons.

"You need to move quickly while remaining calm and orderly," the Administrator squawked on the megaphone. "Get in the backs of the trucks and stay with your spouse. No need to worry, we are only changing locations. You are not in any danger."

Maybe *we* weren't, but *they* probably were. I wondered if the rebel army was close. I turned to Betsy and took a deep breath. It was chilly enough so there was a little vapor in my exhale. I looked in Betsy's eyes and knew I couldn't go on facing them every day, reflecting my own sadness back at me.

"I think this is where I leave you," I said quickly, before I could change my mind. "I'm not going."

"No?" She didn't seem so awfully surprised. Though she's never mentioned it, I think Betsy has seen the change in me since Brother Rita died. She smiled that smile I've come to love over the years. Even the despair which has dogged her the last two and a half years could never fully diminish its abundant warmth. This early in the day, her teeth were as yet unmarked with lipstick.

"No." I took her hand in both of mine and held it to my face. "There comes a time when I draw the line. I've crossed it enough and I'm done." I could feel my mother's spine stiffening in me. It felt like years since I had stood so erect. I turned away, but she suddenly pulled me back.

"I'll miss you," she said. "I hope somehow we'll see each other again."

"Maybe," I said, but I didn't really believe it. She was heading off to who-knows-where while I waited out my future here—and I expected it would be a short one. We hugged for what felt like a half hour until I stepped out of it. I kissed her hand, and then let it go. "Goodbye. Be well."

In the crush of people jammed into the center of the barracks, it was easy to slip away. I didn't even try to hide, but merely walked across the way to my building. No one shouted at me or tried to stop me; they were all busy in their attempts to create order from chaos. I stepped gingerly onto the porch. The front door was unlocked.

   I've never been in the factory office completely alone before. I debated flipping the light switch, but I liked the play of shadows from the trees outside the window, so I left them off and walked behind the counter in the dim morning light. It was so quiet and empty, even my soft-soled shoes announced my presence. I pulled out my chair, and only then realized my plan didn't reach any farther than this. I had no idea what I was supposed to do, or what I was waiting for. So I sat, my hands folded atop my desk.

   Outside, muffled by the walls of the building, I could hear the Administrator giving orders in an unusually calm voice. It was impossible to decipher what he was saying. I strained to hear for a moment or two and then decided it didn't matter. He could have been unlocking the secrets of the universe and it wouldn't affect me in the least. My entire world was this room. My breathing was deep and steady.

   I gotta say, giving up is very liberating.

   I have no idea how much time passed as I sat here doing nothing. There's no clock in the office, and without my computer turned on or the normal morning tasks to occupy me, it's difficult to tell. It might have been ten minutes or half an hour. I watched the shapes of the trees play across the walls. The voices outside were like the buzz of a fly.

I heard the overhead lights crackle to life before the glare bleached the shadows from the room. Someone spoke. I looked across the room, blinking hard; it's possible I may have dozed off. Boss A was standing just inside the door, hand still on the light switch, watching me. He didn't seem angry, just sort of. . .confused more than anything.

"This is the last place I thought you'd be," he said quietly. "Your wife came up as the odd number in your truck. We've been looking for you, Prisoner 34."

"I'm right here." I made no effort to move.

"What, are you saying goodbye to the place?" He glanced at his watch. "Well, say goodbye then and let's go."

"I'm not going," I said. "I'm staying here."

Boss A came around to the back side of the counter and leaned against it, facing me. He crossed his arms across his chest and sighed. He made no effort to reach for the gun strapped to his waist, perhaps assuming its visibility would be threat enough.

"Get up 34," he said, not unkindly. "You can't stay here."

"Why not?" I said. "This place will be abandoned, and I can survive here or I can die. What's it matter to you?" I felt as steely as my chair, our metals now fused and unyielding.

"Because my orders say to withdraw all staff and prisoners, that's why." He actually smiled at me. "I have to follow orders, too. Just like you."

"I'm not following orders," I said, "so you're going to have to leave me here or shoot me. I don't care which."

"Come on now," Boss A said.

Then he addressed me by my real name; I didn't know he even knew it.

"Either way," I said, "I'm just one less fag you have to worry about."

"Don't say that." Boss A made a show of pulling off his rubber gloves and tossing them in the wastebasket next to my desk, as if to prove he had no reason to fear me. "Believe it or not, 34, I actually like you. You're a good worker. Come on now."

He walked over to my desk and stood next to me, putting his bare hand on my shoulder. It was very paternal, even though I'd place him maybe only five or six years older than me, younger than Betsy. "Come on now," he said once again, and the pressure on my shoulder increased, though not by much.

The bullet made a little *ching!* as it shot through the window, flying so fast to its target that the blood from Boss A's head splattered across me before the broken glass had time to hit the floor. He made a little vowel sound, not quite a word, as he was flung back by the force of the shot. I knew he was dead just from the way his body slammed to the floor, with no instinctive effort made to break his fall.

The silence was total and precise for exactly as long as it took me to inhale, and then the atmosphere outside exploded with gunfire.

I put my head down on my desk and closed my eyes. I counted quietly to myself, trying to accurately gauge the length of each second before whispering the next number. The gunfire began to subside at around three hundred, but the commotion never really stopped.

The basso rumbling of tanks, so deep and low I could feel it vibrate in my bones, grew louder and louder until I thought it would knock the office building off its foundation. I heard the groaning creak and snap of wood, and the immediate screams of joy told me our huge green gate was coming down at last. Every sound was so sharp, I could practically track the progress of the rebel army through the hole in the window.

I stayed at my desk—my stubborn streak, now resurrected, refused to let me give in too soon, to hope too high—and didn't move until I counted to one thousand. At last I opened my eyes. The room was dimmer now, the swirl of dust and battle outside creating a dun-colored fog.

Boss A's body lay on the floor, on his back but slightly humped up onto the left shoulder, his unseeing eyes staring straight past me. Almost the very last thing he said was that he liked me. I don't know why he tried to humanize himself like that all of a sudden. It wasn't right for him to do that to me. How dare he do something so simple and nice? Did he think after everything he and I had been through, a scrap of kindness was going to make it all okay? I opened my mouth to tell him so, to reject him for his attempt at humanity, but all that escaped my mouth was a moan so faint it sounded like my last breath of life draining out from a punctured lung.

And then came the tears, unbidden and uncontrollable, so strong and unending a river I could have washed Boss A's blood from my hands. I gritted my teeth uselessly and cursed myself that the tears I'd denied release for so many years should come now at the death of Boss A, when I had refused to cry for so many others, for Dylan, Frederick, Betsy, our baby girl, for all of us here, for the rest of the world, and for myself, too. Me, who maybe deserved my own tears most of all. Instead I wasted them on this man who dared to call me by my real name and tell me he liked me. And I cried until my body had no tears left for anyone.

I pushed the power button on my computer, and while waiting for it to warm up, I crossed the room and slowly opened the front door. I didn't dare risk stepping out into the open and being mistaken for someone other than who I am. So I sat back down at my desk and began to write.

There is a great deal of activity at the barracks while I write this. The original prisoners have all been pulled from the backs of the trucks to make room for the new prisoners, those Officers and Good Guys not shot dead by the rebel army. There are at least a dozen corpses on the ground. If I had tears left, perhaps I'd cry for them as well.

When you told me, Jerry, that I was better off in here than out in the real world, it made me angrier than I have words to express. But not knowing the state of the world I'm being released into, I now wonder if you weren't right.

I don't know if we will ever meet. I don't suppose so, and what would we say to each other if we did? Perhaps we're both better off parting on the best possible terms we can, which is me thanking you for letting me know what was coming, when you were under no obligation to do so. That was very Christian of you, no irony, no quotation marks.

So. Now what?

I know neither who is alive, nor how to find them.

What's left of the city I lived in?

Is my house still standing? Do I get it back?

And of course the question I can barely even type, let alone contemplate: Is Dylan still alive?

When I was a kid, maybe eleven years old, my family went to visit my aunt and uncle in Kansas. I was fascinated by the never-ending horizon, and every time I went outside, it would draw my attention away from whatever game I and my siblings and cousins were playing. In retrospect, it feels like they spent the whole week snapping their fingers in my face to bring me back to reality.

On our last night there, my father and I went out to watch the sunset. I asked him how far away we could see, and he said it was a number so big, he didn't know its name. Instead, he said, we were looking clear out to the ends of the earth.

This state of unknowingness is like that, vast and profound.

I can hear people moving building to building, calling for anyone left to come out, come out. The irony of their choice of words is not lost on me. They assure us that we are all at last safe and free.

They're very close, one building away now. They'll find me soon enough.

Until then, I will sit here and await my deliverance.

Sincerely,

Gordon Raymond Fleck

Made in the USA
San Bernardino, CA
17 October 2014